There's No Such Place
As Far Away

DELACORTE PRESS / ELEANOR FRIEDE

RICHARD BACH

There's No Such Place

As Far Away

Illustrated by RON WEGEN

Published by
Delacorte Press/Eleanor Friede
Bantam Doubleday Dell Publishing Group, Inc.
666 Fifth Avenue
New York, New York 10103

Book design by Ronald Wegen
Text design by Lynn Braswell

Library of Congress Cataloging in Publications Data

Bach, Richard.
  There's no such place as far away.

  1. Wegen, Ronald.   II. Title.
PS3552.A255T5   813'.5'4   78-11244
ISBN: 0-440-50237-3

Manufactured in the United States of America

April 1979

10

Rae! Thank you for inviting me to your birthday party! Your house is a thousand miles from mine, and I travel only for the best of reasons ... a party for Rae is the best and I am eager to be with you.

T began my journey in the heart of the hummingbird you and I met long ago. He was friendly as ever, yet when I told him that little Rae was growing up and that I was going to her birthday party with a present, he was puzzled. We flew for a long while in silence and at last he said, "I understand very little of what you say, but least of all do I understand that you are *going* to the party."

"Of course I am going to the party," I said. "What is so hard to understand about that?" He was quiet, and when we arrived at the owl's home, he said, "Can miles truly separate us from friends? If you want to be with Rae, aren't you already there?"

"Little Rae is growing up and I am going to her birthday party with a present," I said to the owl. It felt strange to say *going* like that, after talking to Hummingbird, but I said it that way so Owl would understand. He, too, flew in silence for a long time. It was a friendly silence, but as he delivered me safely to the home of the eagle, he said, "I understand very little of what you say, but least of all do I understand that you call your friend *little*."

"Of course she is little," I said, "because she is not grown up. What is so hard to understand about that?" Owl looked at me with his deep amber eyes, smiled and said, "Think about that."

"*L*ittle Rae is growing up and I am going to her birthday party with a present," I said to Eagle. It felt strange now to say *going* and *little* after talking with Hummingbird and Owl, but I said it that way so Eagle would understand. We flew together out over the mountains, and soared the mountain winds. At last she said, "I understand very little of what you say, but least of all do I understand this word *birthday*."

"Of course birthday," I said. "We are going to celebrate the hour that Rae began, and before which she was not. What is so hard to understand about that?" Eagle curved her wings into steep dive-flaps and stepped to a smooth landing on the desert sand. "A time before Rae's life began? Don't you think rather that it is Rae's life that began before time ever was?"

"*L*ittle Rae is growing up and I am going to her birthday party with a present," I said to Hawk. It felt strange to say *going* and *little* and *birthday* after talking with Hummingbird and Owl and Eagle, but I said it that way so the hawk would understand. The desert poured by far below us and at last she said, "You know, I understand very little of what you say, but least of all do I understand *growing up*."

"Of course growing up," I said. "Rae is closer to being adult, one more year away from being a child. What is so hard to understand about that?" Hawk landed at last upon a lonely beach. "One more year away from being a child? That does not sound like growing!" And she lifted into the air and was gone.

*S*eagull, I knew, was very wise. As I flew with him, I thought very carefully and chose words so that when I spoke, he would know I had been learning. "Seagull," I said at last, "why do you fly me to see Rae when you know in truth I am already with her?"

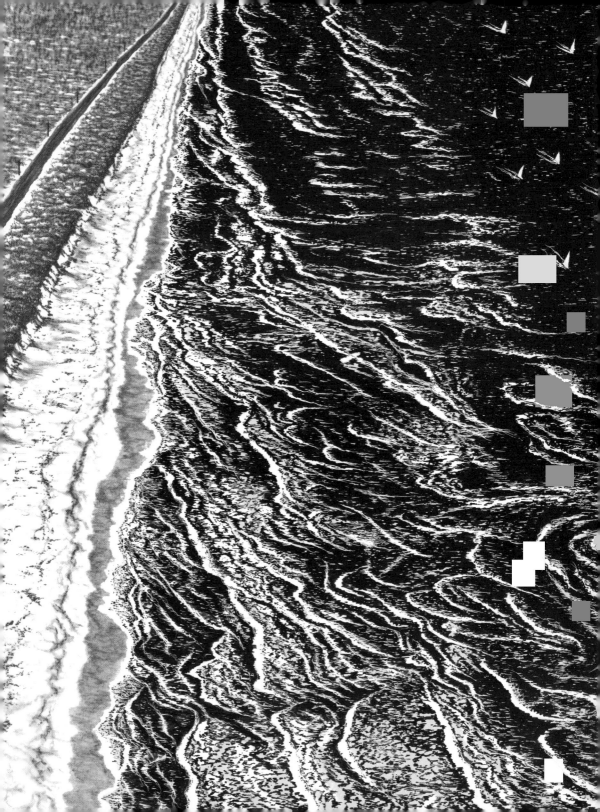

*S*eagull turned down over the sea, over the hills, over the streets, and landed gently upon your rooftop. "Because the important thing," he said, "is for you to know that truth. Until you know it, until you truly understand it, you can show it only in smaller ways, and with outside help, from machines and people and birds. But remember," he said, "that not being known doesn't stop the truth from being true." And he was gone.

Now it's time to open your present. Gifts of tin and glass wear out in a day and are gone. But I have a better gift for you.

It is a ring for you to wear. It sparkles with a special light and cannot be taken away by anyone; it cannot be destroyed. You are the only one in all the world who can see the ring that I give you today, as I was the only one who could see it when it was mine.

Your ring gives you a new power.
Wearing it, you can lift yourself into the
wings of all the birds that fly — you can see
through their golden eyes, you can touch
the wind that sweeps through their velvet
feathers, you can know the joy of going
way up high above the world and all its
cares. You can stay as long as you want in
the sky, past the night, through sunrise,
and when you feel like coming down
again, your questions will have answers
and your worries will have gone.

*A*s anything that cannot be touched
with the hand or seen with the eye,
your gift grows more powerful as you
use it. At first you might use it only
when you are outdoors, watching the
bird with whom you fly. But later on,
if you use it well, it will work with birds
that you cannot see, and last of all you

will find that you'll need neither ring
nor bird to fly alone above the quiet of
the clouds. And when that day comes to
you, you must give your gift to someone
who you know will use it well, and who
can learn that the only things that
matter are those made of truth and joy, and
not of tin and glass.

Rae, this is the last day-a-year, special-time celebration that I shall be with you, learning what I have learned from our friends the birds. I cannot go to be with you because I am already there. You are not little because you are already grown, playing among your lifetimes as do we all, for the fun of living.

You have no birthday because you have always lived; you were never born, and never will you die. You are not the child of the people you call mother and father, but their fellow-adventurer on a bright journey to understand the things that are.

Every gift from a friend is a wish for your happiness, and so it is with this ring.

*F*ly free and happy beyond birthdays and across forever, and we'll meet now and then when we wish, in the midst of the one celebration that never can end.